JUNGLE DOCTOR'S RHINO RUMBLINGS

⑤

JUNGLE DOCTOR'S RHINO RUMBLINGS

Paul White

CF4·K

10 9 8 7 6 5 4 3 2 1

Jungle Doctor's Rhino Rumblings

ISBN 978-1-84550-612-4

© Copyright 1974 Paul White

First published 1974. New edition 1983

Reprinted 1985, 1987, 1988, 1989,1997

Published in 2010 by

Christian Focus Publications, Geanies House, Fearn, Tain

Ross-shire, IV20 1TW, Scotland, U.K.

Paul White Productions,

4/1-5 Busaco Road, Marsfield, NSW 2122, Australia

Cover design: Daniel van Straaten

Cover illustration: Craig Howarth

Interior illustrations: Graham Wade

Printed and bound by Bell and Bain, Glasgow

Mixed Sources

Product group from well-managed
forests and other controlled sources
www.fsc.org Cert no. TT-COC-002769
© 1996 Forest Stewardship Council

FSC

CONTENTS

INTRODUCTION

Paul White learned a great deal from his African friends at the jungle hospital. They befriended him and helped him in his efforts to learn their language, Chigogo.

One of their most important gifts was to teach him how to use animal stories. These stories, or fables, helped to explain abstract thoughts and theological terms.

When the Whites were on their way home from Africa in 1941, they were delayed in Colombo because of German submarine activity. Paul was invited to speak at a girls' boarding school. All the children of non-Christian faiths were sent outside but, hearing laughter from inside, crowded round the windows to see what they were missing. This was the first of many occasions when audiences were gripped by the fable stories.

The first of six fable books appeared in 1955. A menagerie of African animals is used to teach the gospel and how to live the Christian life. In these books you will meet Toto, the mischievous monkey, Boohoo, the hippo who, like the author, suffered from allergies, Twiga, the giraffe and wise teacher, and many others.

They will endear themselves to you as they have to thousands round the globe.

1

I, RHINO

'Are you coming on a safari to the buyu tree to hear a story?' asked the twins, Tali (which means tall and he wasn't) and Kali (which means fierce and he wasn't).

Gulu, whose broken leg was in plaster nodded and they wheeled him down from the Jungle Hospital in the wheelbarrow. Behind them came Elizabeti and Yuditi and between them a tall girl named Lutu whose eyes were bandaged. She had been blind for a very long time, like Liso, her friend – but she was short.

Daudi came striding down from the hospital and sat on the stool which Gulu had brought in the barrow.

'What's the news of the man who was attacked by 'Faru, the rhinoceros?' asked Tali.

'The news is good,' smiled Daudi. 'He will recover; and speaking of Rhino, what is the best thing to do if a rhino chases you?'

'Run,' exclaimed Elizabeti.

'Climb a tree,' shouted Kali.

'Jump to one side,' laughed Gulu, waving his plaster-covered leg in the air.

'Gulu's right,' laughed Daudi. 'Jump to one side it is. Rhino is big, noisy and thinks very much of himself. Listen to a story of the way he threw his weight around in the jungle.'

Snake raised his head and hissed with satisfaction. He watched Rhinoceros admiring his huge shadow which the rising sun spread over the grass slope that stretched down to the river.

'You're big and strong and important,' said Snake, so softly that Rhino thought they were his own thoughts. He bored holes in the clear morning air with his large, spiky horn and a deep rumble came from inside him. 'I am big, I am strong, I am important. I AM RHINO.'

Again Snake whispered, 'Nobody gets in a rhino's way. Nobody tells a rhino what to do. He is quite as important as Elephant.'

Rhinoceros snorted and swished his absurd little tail. Its shadow looked threatening and powerful. His voice came through closed teeth. 'Nobody tells me what to do. Nobody gets in my way. And as for Elephant ... I'll fix anyone who talks to me about him and what he says or does or promises ...'

He thumped his front feet angrily into a pool of mud.

Snake smirked and thought, 'Rhino may be stupid but he is terribly strong. He can be useful to me.' He licked his lips with his forked tongue and hissed. '*Ah*, there he goes.'

Rhino ambled down the path that led to the river. In front of him was the monkeys' palm tree. A massive rhinoceros shoulder crashed into the trunk snapping it like a rotten stick. Toto and Koko, the twin monkeys, landed painfully in the thornbush. Rhino took no notice. He strode on to a place where he found a lump of granite shaped like an over-sized watermelon. On it sat Jojo, the mongoose, who always loved to ask questions.

Rhino stopped. His red eyes gleamed.

'Are you as strong as an elephant?' asked Jojo's eager voice.

Thunder came from inside Rhinoceros. With one prod of his horn he sent Mongoose head over tail and the stone rolling bounding and bouncing down the slope.

Dic-Dic, the antelope, jumped for his life as the stone, hurtling past his head, crashed into a much bigger boulder which rolled into the middle of the road.

Rhino saw Boohoo, the hippo, standing quietly in a water lily pond. With a bellow he ran and jumped, landing *splosh – splash* – SQUELCH! In the very middle. A wave of brown water hit Hippo in the face.

'I'm more important than anyone in the whole jungle and don't you forget it!' roared Rhino. He put his head down and galloped off to the shade of the coconut palms.

Hippo opened one eye. 'Most disagreeable beast! More important than anyone – *eh*? Surely he shuts his eyes to Elephant. It couldn't be that he thinks he ...'

Sliding by in the shadow Snake heard him. Serpent's eye glittered as he silently followed Rhinoceros. 'It's going well,' he hissed. 'My sharp brain can use that mountain of muscle to upset some of Elephant's plans.'

Twiga, Jojo and Dic-Dic stood quietly watching. They saw a movement in the grass.

'Was that Snake?' asked Jojo, fluffing up his fur.

'It was,' nodded Twiga. 'The thoughts of his twisty mind are more dangerous than the poison in his teeth.'

Rhino was resting in the shade. Every thought that crossed his mind started with I, or me, or my. Snake glided up to him and with a sneer in his soft voice said, 'Did you hear that Elephant has plans to bring joy into the hearts of everyone in the jungle?'

'Tell him to tie a knot in his trunk,' rumbled Rhino, thumping angrily into a palm tree.

Nzoka slithered under a rock to dodge the shower of coconuts. After a while he looked out cautiously and whispered in a voice full of persuasion.

Rhino took little notice for a while then he made a noise that was as close to laughter as he knew how and said, 'Tell me again, Nzoka.'

Twiga and the others heard Snake's hissy voice. 'I saw Elephant on the hillside. Why not topple him over into the river? Prove that your horn is better than his trunk. Show the whole jungle how strong you are.'

Rhino puffed out his chest and stalked up the hill rumbling, 'My mind is working very smoothly today.'

'Carefully,' said Twiga, moving towards him. 'Snake's advice isn't worth following.'

'Me! Listen to Snake!!' growled Rhino. 'I do my own thinking.'

Twiga shook his head. 'He is on his way to trouble.'

Far ahead something great and grey and still blocked the track. A snaky smirk spread over Nzoka's face as he watched. Rhinoceros peered into the distance. 'Elephant,' he rumbled. Two huge feet pounded the ground.

'Why should Elephant stand where I want to go?'

Snake whispered, 'He's big. He's important.'

'So am I. I'll show him horns are better than tusks,' interrupted Rhino. Waves of heat shimmered around a boulder-covered hill. Below him the sun shone dazzlingly on the waters of the river. There was the colour of fire in his small eyes. The redder they became the worse they worked.

Rhino snorted and ground his teeth. 'Like his hide.' At the top of his voice he roared, 'Out of my way! Get out of my way! You there! Do you hear me? GET OUT OF MY WAY!' His horn pointed directly towards the great, grey something that showed up sharply against the skyline.

Jojo scurried over and stood right in front of Rhino. 'We know you don't like Elephant. But if you think that's ...'

A bellow from Rhino interrupted him. 'Shut your mouth, will you!'

Jojo didn't move. 'Anyone with half an eye can see that that isn't ...'

'Shut up! SHUT UP! SHUT UP!' roared Rhino, moving forward, his eyes fixed on the hillside. His voice was hoarse. 'Turn your back on me, would you? Take no notice of me, *eh*? Sit in the middle of my path; block where I want to go, would you?' He stopped for breath.

Snake smiled a scaly smile and thought, 'Exactly what I want.'

Down went Rhino's head. Out stuck his horn. He stamped his feet. Dust rose in clouds. The hillside looked red and though he couldn't see it clearly the grey shape made anger boil inside his head. Rumbling furiously, two tons of temper went tearing up the slope. Closer and closer he thundered. Bigger and bigger loomed his target; grey, solid and very large. Rhino pointed his head at its middle and shut his eyes and hurtled forward – WALLOP! – *U-u-g-g-h-h-h!* into a great, grey, granite boulder.

Stars whirled round Rhino's head – big, dazzling, exploding stars. He groaned.

Never had there been such a headache in all the jungle.

'Wow!' said Tali and Kali in the same breath. 'Rhino was very stupid.'

'Watch it,' smiled Daudi. 'Rhino certainly was a skinful of selfishness and pride; but be careful, it could easily happen to you if you turn your back on God and shut your eyes to what He says. Anyone who is travelling God's road and has asked the Lord Jesus Christ to be in charge of his life knows where the world's worst headaches and heartaches come from.'

* * *

What's Inside the Fable?

Special Message: Don't ignore God's instructions. God's way is the best way.

Jesus tells the story of the Pharisee and the Tax Collector: *Luke chapter 18 verses 9 to 14.*

Also he tells the story of the unwise farmer:
Luke chapter 12 verse 16.

Read also about the King who wanted everything and lost the lot: *1 Kings chapter 21.*

King Solomon said there is a way that seems right to a man but in the end it leads to death. *Proverbs chapter 16 verse 25.*

2
ANGER RUNS WILD

'I was sitting under a palm tree,' said Dan. 'Wham! Down came a coconut and did it give me a headache!'

Daudi smiled. 'It's a pity you didn't remember the saying that unpleasant surprises are in store for those who sit under trees. However, cheer up. Your headache was not nearly as bad as the ones Rhino kept on making for himself in the jungle whenever he let his anger boil over.'

'Why shouldn't Rhino be angry if he felt like it?' demanded Kali.

Daudi smiled. 'Anyone can do what he likes. This is called free will. But it's useful to know what will happen. You have seen that there is small comfort and no joy in following rhino wisdom.'

'You should have seen old spiky-nose,' giggled Toto, the monkey. His friends crowded closer. 'He thought a big, grey rock in the middle of the path was the going-away-end of Elephant.' Toto swung by his tail and used all his legs to show exactly what had happened. 'He put his head down. He ran as fast as his stumpy little legs would go and WHAM!'

Twiga's head suddenly appeared amongst them. '*Oh*, small Monkey,' he said, 'he has done that sort of thing before. It is the well-known wisdom of rhinos. Quietly now. He's not very happy today.'

'Happy?' chuckled Toto. 'Old spiky-nose happy? Why he's only a big lump of bad temper inside the thickest hide in the jungle.'

Rhino limped into view. His neck creaked; there was a nagging pain that started between his ears and grew steadily worse when it reached the broken tip of his horn.

'He's been knocked about,' whispered Toto in Twiga's ear.

'You're right,' agreed Giraffe, 'but his pride has been hurt even more than his nose.'

Hippo blinked up at Rhino from the shelter of the water lily pond.

'*Er* – Rhinoceros. I was sorry to hear of your – *um* – accident with that big rock.'

Rhino snorted so loudly that pain stabbed him between the eyes.

Jojo, the mongoose, ran up the side of the great anthill. 'Did you really think it was Elephant?'

Rhinoceros breathed in and out ferociously but said nothing. Stripey the zebra's lips twitched.

Mongoose put his head on one side. 'Does your nose feel better today?'

Stripey smiled a wide zebra smile. At once two red eyes were fixed on him and a rough voice roared, 'Show your ugly teeth at me, *eh*? Sneer at my horn, *ugh*?'

Twiga bent down and whispered, 'Let's move out of the way. When Rhino is angry like this, creatures are hurt.'

Stripey was prancing about on his back heels in a way that made Rhino feel dizzy. 'Stop squirming, will you?' he rumbled. Zebra kicked up his heels. Anger poured into Rhino's brain and he made noises like thunder. With a snort he charged.

Stripey, however, was at full gallop. At first he was well ahead but gradually the ferocious breathing of the great animal drew nearer. Stripey was running in a wide circle. He could almost feel the Rhino's horn brushing his tail. They were coming closer and closer to Jojo's anthill. Rhino's head was down. Through his mind boiled the thoughts, 'I'll hit him! I'll crack him! I'll crush him!' He snorted and ran even faster. Zebra swerved to one side.

WHANG!

'He has done it again,' gasped Dic-Dic.

Twiga nodded. 'Those of his sort do not learn by experience.'

The stars Rhino had seen yesterday were larger than the ones he saw now, but this time the pain was terrible. There was mud in his mouth, mud in his nose and mud in his eyes. With a horrid groan he dragged his horn out of the hard, red earth of the anthill. Through the dust came Hippo's earnest voice, '*Eh* – doesn't your bad temper get you into – *er* – trouble?'

Rhino stamped his feet and ground his teeth. Jojo looked up at him enquiringly. 'Do you like doing that to your nose?'

Zebra laughed.

'I'll rip your stripes into strips,' thundered Rhino. But already Stripey was on the move.

'He's awfully fierce,' said Dic-Dic, 'but the one he hurts most is himself.'

'Did Rhino make that big hole in the *buyu* tree?' asked Jojo.

Twiga nodded. 'As usual he went the way of rhino wisdom. He charged Goon, the baboon. Truly there is much useless anger in Rhino.'

They turned to watch the cloud of dust that raced across the plains. In the middle of it they saw Rhino gaining steadily on Zebra.

Rhino's small eyes blinked in the red dust. 'I'll teach him! It's downhill now. I've got him!' Now he could see four galloping hooves, then the stripes on Zebra's legs. He made a special effort and there, almost in his mouth, was a black and white tail.

'I've got him! I've got him! I'VE GOT HIM!' gloated a voice from deep inside his thick head. Every bit of rhinoceros energy went into his mighty muscles. 'It won't be long now,' he snorted.

It wasn't. As they passed the anthill Zebra swerved again to one side. Rhino was going too fast to stop. He skidded through some of the spikiest cactus in the jungle, tripped, rolled over and over, hurtled over a bank, somersaulted through the air and landed on Hippo.

Boohoo limped out of the water and inspected a large and painful bruise on his hippo hip. As the mud slowly drained out of Rhino's ears he heard a slow sad voice saying, 'Rather a rough and un-dig-nif-ied way to arrive, don't you think, Rhinoceros?'

Rhino lurched out of the pond and turning his back on Hippo stumbled painfully away through the tall grass.

Boohoo blew a long lungful of warm air over his bruised back and said, 'There is more anger in Rhino's head than there is wisdom. That's that sort of anger that does nobody any good, especially yourself.'

'What does God's wisdom say about anger?' asked Kali quietly.

'Here's a list of things,' said Daudi. 'They're worth looking up.'

Tali and Kali did.

* * *

What's Inside the Fable?

Special message: Don't let a bad temper get the better of you.

Read the following verses about anger:
James chapter 1 verse 19

Proverbs chapter 14 verse 17

Proverbs chapter 16 verse 32

Proverbs chapter 22 verse 24

Ecclesiastes chapter 7 verse 9

3

GOOD NEWS FOR BLIND MONKEY

'Do your eyes tell you anything, as I do this?' asked Daudi, turning Lutu, the blind girl, so that the full light of the African sun shone in her eyes.

'There is less darkness when I face this way,' said Lutu.

'That is very good,' said Daudi. 'With God's help we will be able to bring light to your eyes when we operate. But my word to you is: it is much more important that the eyes inside you see than your ordinary ones.'

'What do you mean?' asked Lutu.

'Come down to the buyu tree tonight and listen to the story of small blind Monkey,' answered Daudi softly.

Once upon a jungle day blind Monkey groped his way down the middle of the road, his paws stretched out

in front of him. He stopped. He could sense that a large animal stood somewhere in front of him.

Politely he said, 'Excuse me, are you Elephant?'

Boohoo, the hippo, stopped. '*Eh*, no. Can't you see – *um* – I'm – *um* – Hippopotamus.'

'That's my trouble,' said small Monkey sadly. 'I can't see. I've been blind ever since I went into the sugar cane gardens and fell into the pool of stickiness. My eyes were stuck up and ever since I haven't seen a thing.'

'*Er* – what a pity,' mumbled Boohoo. 'I know a splendid collection of rules to keep you from getting blind in sugar cane – *um* – gardens. *Eh*, you mustn't, *eh* …'

'Please,' said Monkey, 'I very much want to know what Elephant is like.'

'*Eh* – *um* – Elephant. Yes, you go up that hill and you'll – *um* – see some – *er* – coconut palms. Under … '

'But I won't see them. I don't see them. I can't see.'

Monkey's voice was shrill.

'*Oh – er – yes – um –* unfortunate. The second – *um* – rule said, 'When you smell sugar cane don't go any further.'

Boohoo looked around to see if he was understood but small Monkey wasn't there to listen. He had groped his way over the hill.

Snake, Rhino and Hyena saw him coming. Snake slithered forward and made his voice sound very friendly. 'Hullo, Monkey, where are you going and what do you want?'

'I want to know what Elephant is like.'

Rhino snorted and Hyena put his paw over his mouth to stop a giggle.

'Do you, now?' said Snake, trying to make his hiss sound soft. 'Did you know there are lots of ideas around these days about Elephant?'

Monkey spoke in a voice which was very firm for so small an animal. 'I want to know what Elephant is like.'

'Oh, is that all? We can easily fix that.' said Snake and he made signs to Rhino who quietly moved forwards and lay down in the middle of the path.

'Now is your chance. Walk straight ahead,' whispered Snake.

Little Monkey put his paws in front of him and tiptoed forward. He bumped into Rhinoceros who lay, back towards him, completely barring the way. Cautiously Monkey felt the huge back, the tough hide and the big, bumpy bones. 'He's not going to stop me,' thought Monkey and tried to climb over. But with a twitch of his ribs Rhino threw him off.

'Are you Elephant?' demanded Monkey, getting to his feet.

'Of course that's Elephant,' hissed Snake quickly.

Monkey's voice was full of amazement, 'But he's blocking the path. He's only an obstruction. I thought he was kind and would talk to those who talk to him.' With a sigh he felt his way down the great body. 'I will walk round him,' he thought. But as he came level with Rhino's shoulder the big animal rolled over,

26

jerked his head and his horn caught blind Monkey in the chest, knocking him over. He lay gasping for a moment and then struggled towards the other side of the path.

Seeing this, Rhino swished his spiky tail. Little Monkey felt he had been hit by a branch of thornbush. Whimpering with pain he stumbled back the way he had come.

As he disappeared round the corner Hyena sneered, 'That should teach him all he needs to know about Elephant.'

From a distance Dic-Dic, the antelope, had seen all that went on. He came bounding down the path and stopped beside blind Monkey who backed away.

Dic-Dic panted, 'It's all right. I'm Antelope, and I'm your friend. Snake deceived you. You wanted to meet Elephant but he took you to Rhino instead.'

'So it wasn't Elephant at all,' said Monkey.

'It certainly wasn't,' answered Dic-Dic. 'Come with me. Now you'll find out what Elephant is like.' He nudged Monkey with his nose. 'This way. Let's go together.' As they stopped under the umbrella trees he said, 'Here he is.'

Monkey paws touched one of Elephant's back legs. He felt it and sighed. 'Elephant is some sort of large tree.'

'Keep trying,' came Dic-Dic's encouraging voice.

Monkey's paws found another great leg and another and still another. A small smile came over his face. 'He is four trees with warm bark that wobbles.'

Dic-Dic laughed. 'Now feel this.'

Monkey shivered as his paws brushed a long, cold sharp, spear-like thing that seemed to point straight at him. 'Is this Elephant?' he gasped. 'It feels like the thing that hit me when Rhino blocked my path.' He backed away and his head bumped another hard, cold thing just like the first.

'Don't be scared,' urged Dic-Dic. 'Don't run. You're finding out more and more about Elephant all the time.'

In a very small voice Monkey said, 'It's all so hard to understand when you can't see.'

'Those are his tusks. Once Elephant saved me from Hyena and Jackal with them. Now feel this.'

Small Monkey stopped breathing in sheer terror when something like a huge snake touched him. He fell over backwards and then in his panic rushed blindly into the jungle.

But again Dic-Dic was beside him. 'Don't be afraid. That was Elephant's trunk, not a snake. Trunk is the most wonderful nose in the world. Elephant saved my life with it. He lifted me out of a deep and very dark trap. He's strong and kind and gentle. Come back and talk to him. He always answers those who talk to him in the right way.'

'But,' said Monkey, holding on to a small tree, 'are you sure?'

'Of course I'm sure. I know. Come on.' They hurried back to the umbrella trees. Dic-Dic panted, 'There he is. Go on, talk to him.'

Little Monkey swallowed and said huskily, 'Are you really Elephant? Are you strong and ...?'

A big warm voice said, 'Yes, I'm Elephant. Come close and let's talk together.'

'I'm blind,' stammered Monkey.

Elephant touched the small face with his trunk. 'How long have you been blind?'

Suddenly Monkey found it easy to talk. 'There were four of us. We found the sugar cane garden and the great pool of sticky, sweet stuff. We knew we shouldn't have put our faces into it but we did. Ever since our eyes have not seen the light.'

Elephant bent down his great head. 'Would you like to see again?'

Monkey spoke wistfully. 'Yes, but it couldn't happen to me.'

'It could and I will open your eyes for you if you want me to.'

'I do. I want to see very much.'

'Come on, then.' Elephant's trunk lay gently on Dic-Dic's back while Monkey's paw clung to a great tusk as together they walked to the side of the river.

'All you have to do is to trust me,' said Elephant, 'and all will be well.'

Monkey felt water running over his face. He felt the warmness and strength of Elephant's trunk touching his eyes gently. More water and still more water poured down his forehead. Suddenly he felt as if someone was pulling his eyelashes.

'One more trunkful should do it,' said Elephant. 'Gently now.'

Monkey stopped absolutely still. His mouth fell open. The darkness had gone. He could see trees and flowers and Antelope prancing round excitedly. Then he saw four large legs as big as tree trunks. He shyly touched two shining white tusks then his eyes met the twinkling eyes above him.

Little Monkey's voice was full of happiness. 'Now I know exactly what Elephant is like.'

Dic-Dic stood close to him and said, 'Yes. And you know what he can do for you when you trust him.'

There was great happiness in Elephant's mind for even though their voices were soft, Elephant's ears are large and he heard every word

'Yes, you're right, oh, very right,' came a monkey whisper. 'Now I must go and find the other three and bring them to Elephant. It makes all the difference when your eyes are open.'

Hyena snarled. 'All that for a miserable little monkey.'

From among the thornbush Snake hissed, 'That's Elephant for you; always putting his trunk into other people's business.'

'Don't talk to me about trunks; horns are very much better,' rumbled Rhino. 'VERY MUCH BETTER!'

After the story Lutu put her hand on Daudi's arm. 'How can the blindness be taken from my inside eyes?'

'Think of little Monkey,' said Daudi. 'He found Elephant and listened to his words. Hope came into his mind. He asked for help and it was given to him.'

'The eyes inside me begin to see your words,' said Lutu slowly.

* * *

What's Inside the Fable?

Special message: Trust in God. Let him show you what he is really like.

Jesus promises, 'I am the light of the world. Whoever follows me will never walk in darkness, but will have the light of life.' *John chapter 8 verse 12.*

Read what happened to two blind men:
One who lived near Jericho: *Luke chapter 18 verses 35 to 43.*
One who was born blind: *John chapter 9 – the whole chapter.*

4

ELEPHANT IS DEAD

'He seemed to be a clever man,' said Tali, 'and he said that God is dead.'

Daudi lifted his eyebrows. 'Did he now? Why, that reminds me of what happened one day in the jungle.'

'Elephant is dead,' hissed Snake.

'Elephant is DEAD,' howled Hyena.

'Dead! Dead!' echoed Jackal and Vulture.

The sun threw Elephant's shadow on the grassy hillside. Twiga, the giraffe, Dic-Dic, the antelope, and Jojo, the mongoose, thought how huge it looked. They saw the great ears move as jeering voices came again from the dark edge of the swamp. 'Elephant is de-ead! Elephant is de-ead!'

The great shadow had gone from the hill and was moving fast and silently down to the river. Twiga and his companions, listening carefully, could hear a deep, friendly voice that they knew well.

'Do you think he's helping somebody?' asked Jojo. Dic-Dic and Twiga nodded.

Down in the swamp Boohoo, the hippo, splashed importantly to where Hyena and his gang were still chanting, 'Elephant is de-ead.'

'*Uh –*,' said Hippo. 'I think you're mistaken, you know. Why – *um* – I saw his footprints – *er* … '

'He's dead,' hissed Snake. 'Footprints don't mean a thing.'

'*Um* – maybe,' mumbled Hippo, turning his large head. 'But – *um* – listen, isn't that Elephant's voice now?'

Snake hissed so hard that poison dribbled down his chin. Hyena laughed in a way that made Boohoo want to cover his ears, while Jackal and his relations howled in chorus, 'Elephant is de-ead.'

Out of the tall grass waddled Lwalwa, the tortoise. There was a light in his small black eye. He put his head on one side and in rather a squeaky voice said, 'That stuff they're making all the noise about is wrong. I know, because Hyena pushed me over on my back and he and his horrible friends tried to scrape me out my shell and eat me.'

'Oh – *um* – very uncomfortable for you,' panted Boohoo, who had come hurrying up the path.

'What happened?' demanded Jojo.

'Elephant put me back on my feet.'

'Did he hit Snake with his trunk and toss Hyena and Jackal with his tusks?' asked Jojo, jumping from one leg to the other.

There was an odd little smile on Tortoise's face. 'They knew he was coming and disappeared rather quickly. They turned their backs and ...'

'That's a certain way of not seeing Elephant,' said Dic-Dic.

'You're right,' chirped Jojo. 'And how can you hear Elephant's voice if you close your ears?'

'*Er* – yes,' came Boohoo's slow voice. 'And – *um* – if you close your eyes to what he does and – *um* – you won't see it.'

'But you see him and you hear him and you have a warm feeling under your shell when he saves you from great trouble,' said Tortoise.

'But,' demanded Jojo, 'won't Snake and the others that go his way say it didn't happen?'

Tortoise chuckled. 'Dead elephants don't put you back on your feet.'

There was a long silence under the buyu tree, then Daudi said, 'You will meet many people who say that God doesn't exist or that he's dead. Many more live as if He doesn't exist or care.'

There was a nodding of heads.

'What does the Bible say?' asked Tali.

'Look up Psalm 14, Tali. And you, Kali, look up Psalm 53.'

There was a turning of pages and both of them read, 'The fool says in his heart, "There is no God." '

Lutu smiled. 'Twin verses! When God wants to make a thing twice as strong He says it ...?'

'Twice!' cried the twins.

* * *

What's Inside the Fable?

Special message: Don't be a fool. Believe in God.

Read Psalm 14:1

Read Psalm 53:1

Read Isaiah 45:9

Read 2 Samuel 7:22

5

HIPPO PUTS HIS FOOT DOWN

Daudi reached forward to pick an odd-looking yellow toadstool. From the far side of the buyu tree came Kali's voice urgently, 'Great one, don't touch it, it stings.'

Daudi stood back. 'How do you know, Kali?'

'I touched one once,' the boy grinned ruefully.

'Only once?'

His twin brother answered, 'Who has joy in being hurt a second time?'

'You are wise,' nodded Daudi. 'It is wise to hate poison. Now talking of toadstools ...'

One jungle day Toto, the monkey, was strolling under the umbrella trees with a bag over his shoulder. He stopped when he saw Boohoo, the hippo, slowly munching a mouthful of water lily roots, beside the river.

Boohoo hiccoughed happily. '*Er* – delicious,' he murmured, peering down at Toto, and covered his large mouth with his large foot. 'Pardon my hicco hippups – *er* -.' Toto giggled and Boohoo tried again. 'That is – *er* – my hippo hiccups – *er* – I've always suffered from them since the awful day when ...' he placed his foot in front of his mouth and waited. When no hiccough came he smiled slyly. '*Er* – since I ate that – *um* –.' A light came into his eye. He walked briskly to the edge of the swamp and placed his foot carefully and firmly on one particular spot. He put all his hippo weight on this foot and then looked hard at Toto. 'Since I ate – *er* – that – *um* – poison toadstool.' He lifted his foot to show what had once been a yellow umbrella-shaped fungus.

'But why crush it as hard as that? It's only a little one,' said the monkey.

Rhino's voice came harshly from the water lily pond. 'Why crush it at all? It's none of your business what others do or what happens to them.'

Boohoo blinked. 'I shouldn't like anyone to – *um* – suffer as I did. Terrible it was.'

'You thought you were going to die?' asked Toto excitedly.

'*Er* – yes. Then I was afraid I wouldn't. *Um* – awful it was. I hate toadstools and poison.' He hiccoughed again.

'*Ah*- there's anther one.' SPLOSH! Down went his foot.

'And another.' Down it went again. Hippo smiled slowly.

'As you can see, I'm very busy preventing trouble.' He moved to one side – SPLOSH!

Monkey climbed up a rock. 'What sort of trouble?'

'*Er* – toadstools.' Boohoo paused, his foot in the air. 'I told you before, they're poison. I hate poison.'

Toto watched the huge foot land hard on still another toadstool. 'That fixed that,' he chuckled.

'*Er* – yes. That's the way to deal with poison. *Er* – what's in your bag, Toto?'

'It's mine,' said the monkey loudly. 'Keep away from it.'

'*Um* – of course,' nodded Boohoo. 'I was only being friendly. *Er* – where did you find it?'

Monkey held the bag close to him. 'Snake gave it to me. He said there are peanuts in it and a special surprise for me when I open it.'

Rhino came splashing out of the mud. 'Snakes,' he rumbled, 'always talking about snakes and poison. *Pah!*'

He stalked away with his nose in the air.

Hippo's eyes were wide with excitement. 'Snake said that, did he?' He gazed at the bag, 'Peanuts, *eh*? I never heard peanuts make – *um* – a noise like that.'

Monkey sniffed. 'I know peanuts when I smell them. My nose may be smaller than yours but it works better.'

Hippo blinked. '*Er* – what's that sticking through the hole near the top?'

Monkey swung the bag over his shoulder. 'You can't fool me. There's no hole in my bag.'

'Oh – *er* –well – how's that peanut sticking it's – *er* – Toto! That's the first peanut I ever saw that had a head.'

Monkey laughed scornfully. 'Don't try your hippo humour on me.'

Boohoo let out a sigh of relief when he saw giraffe coming towards them. '*Oh – er* Twiga – help quickly – danger – *um*.'

'What's the matter?' asked Twiga.

Toto laughed. 'It's old bumpy here. He's frightened of my bag of peanuts. He can see things poking out of holes that aren't there.'

Twiga bent his neck down. 'Toto, there is a hole in that bag, and there's a small snake pushing his head through.'

'Very funny,' sniffed Toto. However, he took a small look over his shoulder. His mouth gaped. Without hesitation he threw the bag on the ground and bolted up a palm tree.

Twiga nosed the bag cautiously. 'From the wriggling that's going on I'd say there's enough poison in their fangs to kill a treeful of monkeys.'

'Jump on it, Boohoo. Please jump on it,' urged Toto.

Hippo looked up at him and said, 'That's real wisdom, monkey. There is only one way of dealing with snakes and – er – poison. Pity Rhino doesn't understand about this. Now – um – watch.' His large foot came down heavily. He ground the bag and all that was in it hard into the dust and peered up into the palm tree. 'Er – Toto. How unwise you would have been to have kept on carrying that bag when you knew what was in it.'

Daudi stood up and ground the toadstool into the dust with his heel.

Those who listened nodded their heads and talked quietly for a while. Then Daudi said, 'If you know a thing is poisonous, hate it. Don't play with it. Sin is soul poison. Hate it. Don't play with it.'

'But,' said Tali and Kali together, 'everybody knows it is not a good thing to hate people.'

Daudi nodded. 'Listen carefully. God loves sinners but he hates sin. The Bible says, "The fear of the Lord is to hate evil." This is the one time when hating is useful.'

'What does "The fear of the Lord" mean?' asked Kali afterwards.

'I'll write it down for you,' said Daudi.

He did. And what he wrote is on the next page.

* * *

What's Inside the Fable?

Special message: Beware of sin for it destroys. Flee from it.

The fear of the Lord doesn't mean being frightened of God. When you love God you care for Him so much that you want to please Him.

This means you DO what He tells you and you DON'T do the things He says are wrong.

What does the Bible say about the fear of the Lord?

It is the beginning of knowledge: *Proverbs 1 verse 7.*
It is the beginning of wisdom: *Proverbs 9 verse 10.*
It is to hate evil: *Proverbs 8 verse 13.*
Fear the Lord and shun evil: *Proverbs 3 verse 7.*
The fear of the Lord adds length to your life: *Proverbs 10 verse 27.*
The fear of the Lord is a fountain of life: *Proverbs 14 verse 27.*
Better a little with the fear of the Lord than great wealth with turmoil: *Proverbs 15 verse16.*

6

THE DANGER OF SCORNING WARNINGS

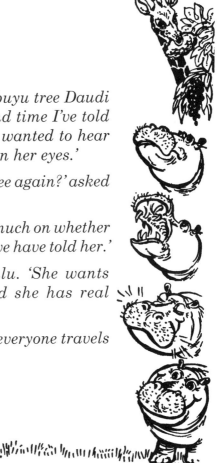

As they sat under the buyu tree Daudi said, 'This is the second time I've told this story today. Lutu wanted to hear it before we operated on her eyes.'

'Will she be able to see again?' asked Yuditi.

'That depends very much on whether she does exactly what we have told her.'

'She will,' said Gulu. 'She wants to see very much and she has real wisdom.'

Daudi sighed. 'Not everyone travels this path.'

It was very hot in the jungle. Everyone was thirsty. Jojo, the mongoose, and Dic-Dic, the antelope, were looking longingly at fruit and berries that grew in the shady trees above them.

Twiga, the giraffe, picked a big, yellow fruit that grew on a tall graceful tree.

'Elephant says, "Eat these. They're delicious. But don't eat any of those." He pointed to a shiny-leafed bush weighed down with glossy, red berries. He shared the yellow fruit with Dic-Dic and Jojo.

'Delicious,' said Mongoose, licking his whiskers.

'It tasted like honey,' nodded Antelope.

Carefully Giraffe picked another as he saw Hippo strolling towards them.

'*Eh* – hot, isn't it?' mumbled Boohoo. '*Um – er –* having a little snack? Oh, I think I'll have one too.' He moved under a cluster of red berries.

'No, don't,' urged Dic-Dic, prancing on his back heels.

'Try one of these,' said Twiga, tossing it in the air.

Boohoo opened his mouth and – WUMPH – the fruit was gone. A slow smile spread over his large hippo face.

'Nice, wasn't it?' said Giraffe. 'Elephant says the yellow ones are sweet and make your stomach sing. But don't ever eat those red berries.'

Rhino came pounding up the path. 'What's that you said? Don't eat this and don't eat that? Take no notice of this "Elephant says" stuff. Be like me, Hippo. I eat what I like when I like and as often as I like.'

Out of the corner of his eye Boohoo was still looking at a cluster of red berries.

'Have nothing to do with them, Boohoo,' said Twiga. 'Elephant knows it's the nature of those berries to make you sick and sore and sorry.'

'*Poof!*' sniffed Rhino. 'Snake told me that Elephant says these things to spoil our fun. Anyhow, it's all a matter of stomachs and mine is the strongest in the jungle.'

'Mine is a very good one, too,' said Hippo very softly, his eyes still on the berries.

'Elephant has words of wisdom,' said Twiga. 'There's a way to do things and a way not to do things in the jungle.'

'Go on,' roared Rhino. 'Tell us this trunk-full of don'ts.'

'It's a good idea to hear them,' said Giraffe, 'and better still to do them. If you come across a place that's like a very small hill covered with tiny pebbles that has lots of holes deep into it, go past it. Don't play there. Don't sit there. Don't rest there whatever you do.'

Goon, the baboon, laughed a monkey laugh. He stood up and swung his way through the trees. From where they stood the animals could see him swaggering along looking this way and that. He stopped in front of a smooth mound covered with tiny pebbles; a mound that had a number of little holes in it. A slow grin spread over Goon's face. He waved his arms and shouted, 'There's nothing I like more than sitting on pebble-covered mounds with holes in them. Why shouldn't I, anyhow? Do what you like when you like and as often as you like.'

'Very soon you will see why Elephant said, "Don't sit on pebble-covered mounds," ' said Twiga.

They watched Goon scratch out a bit of the mound to make a comfortable spot to rest his head. He lay down, stretched and yawned. Suddenly he shrieked, shot into the air and started rushing round in circles.

'Why is he doing that?' demanded Jojo.

Abruptly Goon sat down and clawed at himself with all his paws at once.

'Ants,' replied Twiga. 'Red ants. And how they bite! To sit on an ants' nest is bad, but to stir up an ants' nest is much worse.'

They watched Baboon jump up and bolt through thick jungle, howling at the top of his voice.

'A very – *um* – unwise animal, that,' said Boohoo, shaking his head. 'He – *eh* – should do what Elephant – *um* – says, you know.'

'He's going to the side of the lake,' said Jojo.

'He'll need to watch his step,' said Twiga. 'Down there is a spring, a strange and dangerous place. Something that looks like mist comes out of the ground with the bubbling water. Elephant says, keep away from that place and never put your feet or nose into the water. It's hot.'

Rhino snorted. 'Are you telling ME not to put my feet into that water? Well, I'll tell you here and now, I'll do what I like, when I like. I'm not going to be pushed around just because Elephant says, don't.' His eyes grew red. 'I know my way around. I'm tough. I've got the thickest hide in the jungle. See?'

Twiga raised one eyebrow. 'You saw what happened to Goon when he took no notice of Elephant.' A distant howl came from Baboon as he rolled down the side of a long sandhill.

Rhino grunted. 'I'm different.' He swung around and stamped off downhill.

Boohoo lingered behind the others and looked sideways at a bunch of red berries. He thought how useful it was to have a very strong stomach.

Two stony rock-covered mountains stood side by side with a narrow gap between them. From under a great boulder water gurgled into a shallow pool. Above it was a little white cloud.

'Where did that cloud come from?' asked Jojo.

'It's mist,' grunted Rhino.

'It's neither,' said Twiga. 'It's steam, and steam is very, very hot.'

Rhino sniffed. 'Stop talking rubbish. It's only mist.'

'Don't go near it,' urged Giraffe. 'The steam scalds and burns and blisters.'

'You and your words that nobody understands,' rumbled Rhino. He walked deliberately forward and lifted one big foot.

'Don't!' shouted Giraffe.

Rhino was breathing fast. His eyes were red. His horn stuck out aggressively. 'DON'T! DON'T! DON'T! It's the only word you know. I've lived here all my life and I can look after myself.' SPLASH! He plunged his foot into the bubbling mud and the steaming water. Something that stung like a wasp landed on Dic-Dic's nose. Stripey, the zebra, kicked up his heels in alarm. Twiga quickly brushed a hot lump of mud off his foreleg.

Rhino's lips were rolled back in a sneer. 'I'm tough. This does nothing to me. *Ye-ow!*' The heat started to find its way through his skin. With a rumbling yell Rhino pulled his leg out of the mud and struggled off, groaning, into the coolest parts of the jungle.

Boohoo shook his head. '*Er* – pig-headed, isn't he? After all the – *um* – trouble Elephant went to explain you'd – *er* – think Rhino would have enough sense to – *er* –' He paused and noticed that the others were watching Goon climb up the steep side of a hill looking for an anteater to help him with the ants he couldn't reach.

No one was looking at Boohoo, whose mouth was watering. He moved towards a red berry bush murmuring, 'With a strong stomach like mine a few won't matter. Elephant must have been talking about big bunches.' CRUNCH! His lips closed over a bunch he felt was very small indeed. His jaws hardly moved as he chewed. 'Interesting flavour,' he thought. He swallowed and there was a sudden sour feeling inside him.

As Goon disappeared over the hilltop, Jojo turned round and shouted, 'Look at Hippopotamus!'

Boohoo sat propped against the trunk of a *buyu* tree, groaning and massaging his middle with his front feet. As they watched, perspiration ran down his nose and his skin turned a peculiar green colour. 'Oh dear,' came his voice sadly. 'It's awful.'

'He's been eating red berries,' said Dic-Dic.

Jojo nodded. 'And they're very busy inside him.'

'It was only a very little bunch,' gulped Hippo. He struggled to his feet. '*Er* – look out everybody. I'm going to be ... I'm going to ...' The animals hurriedly moved round the *buyu* tree as Hippo said a sad farewell to the red fruit which he'd been told would certainly produce this unhappy result.

Quietly Twiga said, 'Today should help us all to remember that the do's and don'ts of the Great One of the jungle are worth not only listening to but obeying.'

When the moon had risen Daudi stood beside Lutu's bed.

'Did they like the story?' she asked in a whisper.

'Yes, they did.'

The girl spoke very softly. 'I want to see again. Don't fear, Bwana Daudi, I won't scorn any warnings.'

'That is the path to travel,' nodded Daudi. 'Don't follow rhino wisdom, baboon belief, and the confused thinking of hippos. Go that way and the results are easy to see.'

'To understand,' whispered Lutu.

'To see and understand.' There was confidence in Daudi's voice.

'God says if we do what He tells us in the Bible we can have lives with purpose and joy in them.'

'How does He tell us?' asked Lutu.

'He gave us ten special instructions and they're nothing like the rules Hippo thinks up.'

* * *

What's Inside the Fable?

Special message: Listen to God's Word and obey it. Don't ignore his warnings.

The first four rules say DO and the last six say DON'T. They're in *Exodus chapter 20.*

Jesus summed them all up in the two DO's which cover the lot. See *Mark chapter 12 verses 29 to 31.*

7
THE COOL POOL

Those that listened were more than interested in a watermelon that Daudi was cutting up.

'The twins aren't here,' said Gogo. 'Shall I find them?'

'Please,' nodded Daudi.

Before long he was back with Kali and Tali, neither of whom seemed very happy. They looked at the melon, glanced at each other and then were conscious that Daudi's eyes were fixed on them.

It was clear to them both that he knew they had taken and eaten one of his melons.

Kali said softly, 'I'm sorry, great one. Forgive me.'

'Me too,' mumbled Tali.

Daudi smiled. 'Yes, I will. Now eat up and listen to the story of the Cool Pool.'

Butterflies of many colours flitted in and out of the sunlight and shadows.

Rhino snorted as he came limping down the path. His foot throbbed where he had put it into the hot spring. His small brain inside his hard, hard head throbbed in sympathy as he thought of Elephant.

Out of the deep shade peered Boohoo, the hippo. '*Um* – careful where you're going. That's Elephant's special cool pool. The best – *um* – drinking place we – *eh* – have. *Um* – very nice it is – *er* …'

Rhino stopped. His small eyes saw the reflection of Giraffe and Mongoose and Antelope in the calm, clear water. They grew red as they saw the flowers round the edge of the grassy bank and the smooth, soft grass. He started, 'Cool, did you say COOL?' His leg was painfully hot.

'*Er* – yes – very,' nodded Boohoo. 'Not at all like the – *um* – place you – *er* – walked into the other day.'

'Didn't you see that small cloud of steam?' demanded Jojo.

Rhino swung round. 'Blaming me, are you?'

'*Um* – *er* –,' remarked Boohoo. 'So it was Tembo, the elephant's fault, was it?'

Rhino turned up his lip. There was a sour sound in his rumble. 'Big, strong, wise Elephant! "Listen-to-what-I-say-and-do-it" Elephant! *Pah!*'

Hippo had an unusually tough sound in his voice. 'You be careful, Rhinoceros. One day you'll need Elephant's help. You won't deserve it then, and you don't deserve it now.' He paused for breath and Dic-Dic whispered, 'He said more words in that breath than I've ever heard him – and not a single '*um*'.'

Rhino angrily tore chunks out of the grassy bank with his horn. Hippo went on. 'Why he cares about creatures like you is beyond my comp – *er* – comphre – *er*,' he gulped. 'I can't – *um* – understand it.'

'So Elephant cares about me? *Pah!*' Rhino lurched into the water. 'I'll do what I want, when I want and any way I want.'

He plunged his head under water and using his horn like a plough did his best to bring the bottom

of the pool to the top. He surfaced again, made a rude noise that sent twisted ripples over the muddy water, then he stamped and splashed his way up the bank.

Rhino stood glaring around him. The jungle echoed with his rumbling. 'Clear, cool pool, *eh*? It's a mud-hole now!' He snorted up at Giraffe. 'And when you see Elephant, tell him to tie a knot in his trunk.'

He galloped off through the thorn-bush and nearly crashed into Elephant. He swerved, sneered over his shoulder, and deliberately turned his back on Tembo.

Twiga and the others looked sadly at the mess that Rhino had made. They all had the same thought in their minds.

'Let's tidy things up,' said Giraffe.

'*Er* – yes. I'll use my – *um* – feet to level things off. Very useful, feet like mine.'

Twiga stretched his long neck over the pool and lifted twigs, weeds and grass out of the middle. Dic-Dic did the same round the edges while Jojo nosed back the flowers and ferns that had been uprooted.

Standing carefully on three legs, Boohoo used one large foot to smooth out Rhino's footprints and skidmarks. The corners of his large mouth turned up. '*Er* – useful we are. It's nice to be able to please Tembo.'

Next morning when they came to drink, the water was clear and cool. The small flowers were growing nicely. There was very little sign of Rhino's dirty work.

'Isn't this a lovely place?' said Mongoose.

'It is,' said Dic-Dic. 'And it's ours because it's Tembo's and we're his friends.'

Koko, the monkey, came scampering down the path. She stopped, picked up a paw full of pebbles and started tossing them into the shapely pool. She liked the plopping noises they made. Her gleeful chattering suddenly changed to a yell as something very large closed firmly round her tail and dragged her back.

A peculiar muffled voice said, '*Eh!* Stop it, monkey. That's Elephant's cool pool.' Boohoo backed away three hippo-lengths and then opened his great lips.

Koko tweaked out her tail. 'So what, you big brutal – bumble-footed beast? I'll do what I like, when I like and how I like.'

'*Er* -,' said Boohoo, ' – you've been listening to him, *eh*? Well, I was just stopping you from – *er* – doing to that beautiful drinking place what you knew you shouldn't.'

Koko put out her tongue at him and scampered up a palm tree. When the others had walked down the path and she thought no one was looking she started to throw lumps of mud into the cool pool. Then she broke off a palm leaf and swished it here and there till the water was brown. Giggling to herself she tossed the palm leaf into the pool and pulled up the flowers that grew near the edge and threw them in, roots and all.

As Koko stood back to admire her work, over her shoulder she saw Elephant standing and watching. She shot up a tree and leaped from limb to limb till there was no jump left in her legs or in her tail. Exhausted, she crawled into the hollow of a *buyu* tree and hid.

Days went by and it was Koko's birthday. She chortled with joy and swung by her tail singing monkey melodies:

'Happy birthday to me
For I live up a tree,
Happy Birthday for Koko,
There'll be presents, you'll see.'

At that moment Twiga's head appeared beside her. 'Happy birthday, Koko.'

Small Monkey jumped onto Twiga's neck and chuckled, 'Today's my latest birthday. I have two every year now. It helps me to grow up quicker.'

'That's monkey wisdom,' smiled Twiga. 'I came to tell you that Elephant wants to see you.'

Koko jumped down and bolted.

Under the umbrella tree she met Dic-Dic. 'Koko, happy birthday. Here's a present for you.' Wedged between his small horns was a yellow jungle fruit. Koko grabbed it.

'Thank you, Dic-Dic, it's lovely.' She said nothing for a while as her mouth was too full. And then, 'Birthdays are marvellous! I think I'll have three every year in future.'

Dic-Dic laughed. 'Oh, did you hear that Elephant is looking for you?'

'What does he want me for?' she asked, with her face as innocent as she could make it.

'He wants to give you a present,' said Dic-Dic.

Jojo interrupted. 'But you don't deserve it. Think of what you did to Elephant's cool pool.'

'I didn't,' started small Monkey. And then she remembered that Elephant had seen her.

She walked on down the path feeling sadly that this wasn't being as good a birthday as she thought. Things changed suddenly when she saw Hippo coming up the path with a smile all over his face.

'*Er* – many happy – *um* – oh – *um* – Koko, I have a watermelon for your birthday.'

'Thank you, Boohoo, I love melons. I was thinking of having four birthdays a year from now on.'

But Hippo wasn't listening. He was licking his lips. '*Um*,' he said. '*Er* – it isn't easy for a hippo to carry things, so I – *er* – put it in my – *er* – mouth and – *um* – absent – *um* – mindedly – *er* – I forgot and chewed it. Lovely flavour, that melon. *Um* – delicious.'

Koko stood looking at him with her paws on her lips. 'You ate my melon?' she shouted.

Hippo nodded. 'As I – *um* – said before, delicious it was. But – *um* – cheer up, Koko, it's the thought that matters. I – he – *oh* – did you hear that Elephant wants to see you?'

Monkey made a face at him and hurried on.

'She didn't deserve that melon,' mumbled Hippo, shaking his head. 'I shouldn't have given it to her.'

Round the corner trotted Koko and nearly bumped into Elephant. She stopped, tried to run away, but her legs didn't seem to be able to carry her. Her mouth felt dry. '*Er – um,*' she spluttered, and in her mind she saw a picture of the cool pool all mud and mess and Elephant looking at her.

'Happy birthday,' came Elephant's big, friendly voice.

Koko looked at the ground and mumbled. 'Thank you.'

'Look,' said Elephant. 'I have a present for you.'

Koko glanced up and saw a bunch of beautiful, ripe bananas being held out towards her. She stretched out a paw and then shook her head. In a very small voice she said, 'I made a mess of the pool, Tembo. I'm sorry.' There was a big pause. 'I don't deserve to be given a present.'

'But this is my gift to you because I like you and want to do something for you. When you were sorry I forgave you, but even before that the bananas had been picked for you.'

Koko was feeling very small inside. 'Thank you, Tembo.' She looked at the bunch of bananas. It was almost as big as she was. 'Thank you very much.' She smiled. 'I'm going back to the pond to clear up as well as I can.'

Elephant's eyes were smiling. Koko didn't see. She was still feeling very small.

As she carried her bunch of bananas down the jungle path she thought, 'I'll share Tembo's gift with

Hippo and Twiga and Dic-Dic and Jo-Jo – and Rhino, too, if I meet him.'

She did, and it was the best birthday she'd ever had.

'Think of a man who has never tasted a melon,' said Daudi. 'He never will know what he is missing till he splits one open and tastes it.'

Heads nodded in agreement.

Daudi went on, 'There is a word with wonderful things inside it. Understanding it is like getting your teeth into the best melon there ever was.'

'What is the word, great one?' asked Gulu.

'It is GRACE, and it means being offered a tremendous gift absolutely free.'

'A gift you don't deserve.'

'A gift you can't buy.'

'A gift you can't earn by doing things or not doing things.'

'What is the gift?' queried Gogo.

' Through what Jesus did God gives us His loving forgiveness, His mercy, His mighty kindness, and life that is ours with Him forever.'

'Here it is all drawn up like a road sign to heaven.'

He handed them a piece of paper. (See over the page for what was written on the paper).

Kali and Tali waited until the others had gone, then Kali said, 'Great one, we didn't deserve that watermelon.'

'And you forgave us for stealing,' chimed in Tali.

'I like you very much, that's why I gave and forgave,' smiled Daudi.

'I'm beginning to understand grace now,' nodded Kali. 'We didn't deserve anything but you still gave.'

They started to pick up bits of melon rind that the others had thrown about.

'You know, Kali, we did deserve something, but I'm glad we didn't get it.' Said Tali quietly. 'It's good to be forgiven.'

* * *

What's Inside the Fable?

Special message: God's salvation is a free gift which we don't deserve.

Read in *Ephesians chapter 2 verse 8:*

By grace we are saved – we don't deserve God's gift of forgiveness.

Through faith – we must believe what God says.

This is not our own doing – not because of works.

It is the gift of God – entirely free.

8

ELEPHANT SAID

Gulu's leg was out of the plaster and he was walking with the help of a stick. The barrow was being wheeled down and in it was Lutu, propped up on a pillow and covered with a blanket.

Under the buyu tree sat Dan looking glum. 'Why did Elephant say, Don't do this and Don't do that? Didn't he ever say, Do?'

Daudi smiled. 'For those who listen he constantly shows them the way much more often with do's than don'ts. Dic-Dic found how useful this could be.'

'*Um* – what goes on down there?' said Hippo to himself as he climbed the hill that overlooked the waterfall. He saw Hyena and three jackals sneaking along different paths far below him.

Behind him came the voice of Twiga, the giraffe. 'Boohoo, look down there. They're after Dic-Dic, the antelope.'

'*Er* – yes,' mumbled Boohoo. 'And I – *um* – said to myself, 'It's just as well that – *um* ... O – *oh*, look at that.'

Dic-Dic, the antelope, was grazing on a patch of green grass not far from the river. He looked up at the blue sky and watched busy little clouds hurrying about. He thought, 'It's wonderful to be alive. How peaceful everything is.'

At that very moment, from behind him came a loud hiss and he saw Nzoka, the snake, poised to strike. Startled, Dic-Dic leaped over an anthill and bounded down the path to the river. On each side was dense undergrowth and thorn-trees. He swung round a bend. Blocking his way were three jackals. Moving like lightning, he shot down a narrow sidetrack where a grinning Hyena waited for him.

Dic-Dic plunged sideways through thorns and nettles to a long strip of sand that stretched far out into the river. He stopped to look back and saw Snake move between him and the bank. Soon the jackals joined him and Hyena shambled past them and came towards him.

On top of the hill Hippo shook his head. '*Er*, nasty. They're trying to drive little antelope into the river. They'd – *um* – like him to fall over the waterfall.'

'Yes,' agreed Twiga, the giraffe. 'That's exactly what they want. It's certainly just as well that ...' He stopped and looked down.

Dic-Dic saw he was trapped. The roar of the waterfall was terrifying. The ring of sneering faces that slowly moved closer filled him with fear. 'Oh,' he breathed, 'if only Elephant was here.'

As if in answer, Elephant's voice came strongly. 'Dic-Dic, you must cross the river. I'll be near you all the time.'

Boohoo held his head on one side. '*Eh* – that's Elephant's voice. Can you hear it, Twiga?'

'Very clearly,' said Giraffe. 'But does Dic-Dic?'

As he spoke they saw Dic-Dic's head nod and nod again.

'All will be well if you do what I tell you,' came Elephant's voice again. 'Run through the shallows towards the round rock, then follow the ridge of white water.'

Dic-Dic didn't hesitate. He jumped into the river. Behind him he saw Hyena's shadow. Spray splashed into his eyes but his feet touched rock. He moved fast. Without warning he was in deep water and being swept along by the stream. In front of him was the ridge of white water. He swam with all his strength and stumbled onto soft gravel. He struggled to his feet.

'Well done,' came the big, encouraging voice. 'Go carefully ahead and you'll find a sandbank going a long way across the river. Climb onto it and rest for a while.'

Dic-Dic set his teeth. There was a hot feeling in his chest. He was dizzy and it was all he could do to keep his head above the surface. At last his feet touched the sloping sand. The water above it was shallow. He stood panting for a minute. His legs trembled as he walked cautiously along the sandbank. The thunder of the waterfall made him shudder. There was river all round him. It slid past, deep and powerful. Dic-Dic looked behind him. Swimming through the white water and climbing up onto the sandbank came Hyena hungrily licking his lips.

From surprisingly close came Elephant's voice. 'On now, Dic-Dic. Just below the surface in front of you is a long log. It's slippery. Go carefully, and you'll come to a grey, level place. Stand firmly on this.

Under the fast-moving water Dic-Dic saw the outline of the log. His heart was in his mouth, he put one foot on it and hoof by hoof moved forward putting his weight cautiously on each leg as he edged forward. The strength of the current was tremendous. Fear told him, 'If you fall in you will be swirled over the cliff like a leaf.'

Then he saw the grey place.

From the sandbank came Hyena's voice, 'What will you do when the log ends? *Eh*? You're not strong enough to swim against that current. Just look at it. *Look at it!*'

Dic-Dic glanced over his shoulder. One foot slipped. The water swirled around his knees. He stumbled and with a splash he went under. He felt himself being swept towards the waterfall. His head came up. 'Help!' he spluttered.

At once something warm and strong gripped him and held him up while great legs swam powerfully to the bank.

'It's you, Tembo,' panted Dic-Dic. 'You were close all the time.' Elephant nodded and placed him safely on the dry ground. 'The top of your head was the grey place. You were at the end of the log.'

'Yes,' said Tembo. 'There was no time that I wasn't able to save you both from the river and from Snake and his evil friends.'

Dic-Dic rubbed his head against Elephant's trunk. 'Thank you, Tembo. You said if I obeyed you would rescue me.'

He looked up into a smiling pair of eyes and heard the deep voice. 'The day you were caught in the trap you trusted me and did what I said. You did it again today. I'm always close to you so keep on trusting me and doing what I say.'

Up on the hill Hippo was peering down wide-eyed. '*Um* – he's safe.'

'Oh, yes, he's safe,' said Giraffe. 'Dic-Dic has learned Elephant's two simple rules: Trust and Obey.'

Daudi smiled, 'God's book tells of people who trusted and obeyed and of those who didn't.' He held up a piece of paper. 'Look up these stories and see which is the way of wisdom.'

* * *

What's Inside the Fable?

Special message: Trust and obey the Lord God. It is the wisest thing to do.

Jesus tells about two men: *Matthew chapter 7 verses 24 to 27.*

Jonah was the man who was told to go *here*, so he went *there*, and found himself in deep trouble. Read the whole book of Jonah ... you'll enjoy this adventurous story!

9
KNOTS UNTIED

'It's very thin stuff,' said Daudi, holding up a ball of string.

'Thin but very strong. Two twists and it's very hard to break it. Ten twists and you're tied up. Listen to my riddle. What is it that looks easy to escape from but steals your freedom?'

Daudi held up his hand. 'Don't tell me till you hear what happened one day in the jungle.'

'It's very thin,' said Toto, the monkey.

'One of the most slender vines in all the jungle,' giggled his twin sister, Koko.

'What are you going to do with it?' asked Stripey, the zebra.

'You're very strong, aren't you?' smiled Koko.

'Of course I am,' snorted Zebra.

'The vine tells you how strong you are,' smirked Koko. 'Just wind it round your legs, like so, and see if you can break it.'

Six twists were in place. Stripey gave a small kick and the vine broke.

'Very good,' shouted the monkeys, clapping their hands. 'You are a particularly strong animal.'

'Try again,' urged Zebra, who felt very pleased with himself. They did; and worked fast and hard. Stripey found he was so firmly bound that he couldn't walk. He glared at his tied-up legs and started to struggle and squeal.

'He'll tangle his stripes soon,' giggled the monkey twins, as they watched Stripey kick violently, roll on his back and snap at the tough vine which bound him tightly with his teeth.

'*Er* – Zebra – ' said Boohoo who was walking past, 'don't you think it's – *um* – rather hot to do that sort of thing?'

Stripey panted, 'Help me, Boohoo. The monkeys have tied me up. I can't undo myself.'

'*Ooh*,' mumbled Hippo, 'uncomfortable and – *um* – difficult, *eh*?' A smile crept over his large face. '*Er* – *um* – I'll bite through that stuff that's round your legs. My teeth are bigger than yours.' He opened his mouth wide and ambled closer.

Zebra squealed in alarm. Boohoo paused, '*Oh* – perhaps you're right. I'll go and look for Elephant. He's the one for this kind of trouble.'

When he had lumbered out of sight the twins returned and made up monkey rhymes about zebras and stripes and vines and knots.

From behind them came Snake's admiring voice. 'Skilful work, monkeys. Splendidly done. How many times did you twist that stuff round his legs?'

'He did ten and I did ten,' gurgled Koko. The monkeys smirked at each other and said together, 'But we can do better than that.'

'I'm sure you can. Wouldn't it be smart to tie up that old skinful of sadness, Boohoo?' hissed Snake. 'You'll need at least fifty twists to hold him.'

The monkeys patted each other on the back and watched Hippo hurry importantly along the path beside Elephant. His voice came puffily, 'There he is, Tembo, tied up with monkey vines, *er* – that is – *um* – monkeys tied up his vines with legs – *oh* – *er*.' He blinked and said, '*Er* – *oh* ...'

There was a twinkle in Elephant's eye as he came close to Stripey. 'I'm tied up and I want to be free,' gasped Zebra.

Tembo's trunk moved swiftly. The vines snapped and Stripey stumbled to his feet and walked unsteadily away.

Boohoo mumbled, 'Surprising that – *um* – Zebra couldn't break those little vines.' He yawned and walked slowly into the shade.

Snake slithered into the sunlight. He looked up at the monkeys. 'Clever ones,' his voice was very syrupy, 'now's your chance. Tie cunningly. Remember. He's as strong as Rhino.'

Hippo lay snoring gently in the mud with his front legs up under his chin. Nimbly, the monkey twins

bound those legs with fifty twists of vine and made sure the knots were very firm. Then they tickled Hippo's nose with a long piece of fluffy grass.

Hippo sneezed, sending up a fountain of water. He sneezed again as he struggled to his feet, tripped, and fell head first into the water lily pond. With much difficulty he struggled up the bank and stood inspecting his front legs carefully. '*Um* – how extraordinary. They're tied – *um* – up.'

For a long time he tried to free himself. Then he sighed and shook his great head. The small monkeys jumped gleefully from tree to tree and watched him stumble his way along the path to find Elephant.

Snake's voice interrupted monkey laughter. 'The very best joke of the lot would be to work on Rhino. At this very moment he is up on the side of the hill.'

'We know,' shouted the monkeys. 'He'll be admiring his shadow and saying, "I'm big, I'm strong, I'm powerful." '

They raced up the hill gathering armfuls of thin, tough vine as they ran. At the top they found Rhino stabbing holes in the air with his great sharp horn, and swishing his bristly tail.

Very politely the monkeys came close and Toto said, 'Excuse me, but can you tell me if rhinos are stronger than hippos?'

'What? What's that you said?' roared Rhino, so loudly that the monkeys bolted up a big tree.

Toto hung by his tail and said most respectfully, 'Zebra said that for his size he was much stronger than Hippo. He also said that Hippo was as strong as you are.'

Rhino was furious. His rumbling turned into a bellow. 'That miserable striped apology for a donkey. What does he know about rhinoceros strength? I will show you what it's like. Try tying MY legs with your stupid vines!'

'Are you sure you want to do this?' hissed Snake. 'After all you're Rhino. Do you need to prove ...?'

'Get on with it!' snapped Rhino putting his front legs together.

Quickly Toto and Koko wound the vine round the strong stumpy legs. Rhino's little eyes were scornful.

'Twenty turns. That's what tied up Zebra,' shouted Koko.

'Don't insult Rhino,' hissed Snake.

'*Pah!*' sniffed Rhino, stretching his muscles. PING went the vine. Quickly Toto and Koko were at it again.

'You're wasting your time,' rumbled Rhino.

But monkey paws went on briskly. At last Toto tied a knot.

'Fifty turns. That should stop any hippo.'

Rhino's lips curled. 'Hippo, did you say? Don't talk to me about hippos. Anything Hippo can do I can do better.'

He bent his great knees. At first nothing happened. He took a deep breath. His muscles bulged. PONG! Bits of vine flew in every direction. A deep rumble of satisfaction came from Rhinoceros.

Toto looked admiringly at him and sighed. 'It's almost a waste of time to test strength like yours.' He tilted his head on one side. 'Nothing could tie you down.'

While he was talking Koko ran off for more vine. Snake moved along beside her in the tall grass, saying softly, 'Use thicker stuff and tie his back legs as well.' When he was back coiled on the flat rock he hissed angrily to see Elephant in the distance watching all that was happening.

Koko threw down an armful of vine. 'One more try,' laughed Toto.

Rhino's small, bone-surrounded brain was so full of thoughts of his power, size and importance that he did not notice fast-moving monkey paws.

Round and round went the vines. Time after time they tied and retied firm knots. 'Sixty,' whispered Toto, who was working on the back legs. 'Another twenty and we've got him.'

After a time Toto came round to the head end of Rhino and held up a loop of vine. 'Thin, isn't it? Silly even to think that stuff like this could hobble a magnificent animal like you ...'

Rhino's mind came back from thoughts of himself and what he could do. He heaved with his shoulder and kicked with his legs. The muscles stood out in his great neck but nothing happened. He snorted, 'Why doesn't this wretched thin stuff break?' He sweated and strained but still nothing happened.

The monkeys giggled and ran away. A creepy feeling started to spread under Rhino's hide. Could it be that his stuff was stronger than he had thought? With growing alarm he battled to free himself. He wrenched and tugged. He slashed with his horn but his bonds only cut in more deeply. In desperation he made a huge effort, lost his balance and fell with a thud that shook the nearby jungle.

He lay panting. The sun beat down. Vultures started circling. They saw a look in Rhino's eyes that had never been there before. He lay in the dust, his flanks heaving.

Snake, comfortably coiled up on a warm rock, hissed softly with satisfaction as he watched hyenas and jackals creep closer. He delighted to bring fear and pain and misery.

Rhino's mind was plagued with the thought that the thin vine was stronger than he was. He shivered as more vultures kept arriving. He rolled over, his back touching a tall anthill. In panic he beat his legs wildly against it. Dust rose in clouds. Great lumps of red earth broke off and thudded to the ground, but do what he would, Rhino's legs were as tightly bound as ever. Vultures fluttered above his head and the hyenas again moved closer.

'It's hopeless,' gulped Rhino. He heard the wind blowing through the tall grass, the flapping of great wings, the hungry panting of the hyenas, and then the angry hissing of Snake which grew louder and louder. Vaguely came the sound of great feet hurrying up the hill. The noise of vultures and the others was suddenly gone and everything was quiet.

Wearily, Rhino opened his eyes. Looking at him were Elephant and Giraffe. Hope came slowly into Rhino's mind. Slowly he realised that Elephant could set him free. He tried to speak but his mouth was too dry. He tried again and heard his own voice, cracked and husky, saying, 'Help me, Elephant. Help me. I can't ... I can't ...'

At once he was shaded from the sun's heat and something very strong and capable was working on his legs. The terrible tightness grew less. He could move and stretch. He was being helped back onto his feet.

Snake was hissing loudly. 'You're free. But you didn't need his help. A few more minutes and your own strength would have done it. You didn't need him.'

Giraffe bent his long neck. 'Rhino, when you found it was hopeless and you couldn't help yourself, Elephant set you free.'

Rhino looked up and saw Elephant looking towards him and inviting him to go with him up the narrow path. He muttered something that sounded like, 'Thank you, Tembo.'

Angrily, Snake watched Rhino limping uphill beside Elephant. He hissed, 'Yes. Go with him now, but there will be plenty of other days for me to get you back into your old way.'

'You know better than that,' said Giraffe quietly. 'You'll never get him back while he keeps close to Elephant.'

'The name of the vine was sin,' said Tali and Kali together.

'Right,' nodded Daudi, 'Sin doesn't seem to tie you up but the more you sin the more it binds. The frightening thing is you cannot free yourself from it. But Jesus is the one who takes away your fear and gives freedom and forgiveness.

'God tells us in the Bible, if the Son – that's the Lord Jesus Christ – sets you free, you will be free indeed.'

'Where does he say that?' asked Gogo. See below:

* * *

What's Inside the Fable?

Special message: Jesus is the only one who can free us from the guilt and power of sin.

Jesus sets us free: *Romans chapter 8 verse 2.*

Jesus talks about FREE MEN and SLAVES. *John chapter 8 verses 31 to 36.*

What Jesus does for people is in *Hebrews chapter 2 verses 14 to 18.*

King David wrote a song about freedom: *Psalm 40.*

10
RHINO WITH A DIFFERENCE

'Which way did Rhino go?' asked Gulu.

'Rhino had two choices: to go Elephant's way or not to go.'

'What happened?' asked Lutu, the girl with the bandaged eyes.

Rhino had been thinking. He stood in a cool part of the jungle and blew gently on his front legs where the vines had cut in deeply. He felt a strange warm feeling inside him. He looked up to see Dic-Dic standing beside the great anthill.

'Elephant was very gentle when he undid your legs?'

'He was,' said Rhino, and all the rumble had gone out of his voice. He held up one leg. 'I couldn't get away from that stuff by myself.'

'You're right,' nodded Dic-Dic. 'You were tied up very, very tightly. Elephant saved me, too, when I was in the hunter's trap. I tried and tried but I couldn't get out by myself. He lifted me out. All I had to do was to hold onto his trunk. Let's go and talk to him now.'

Snoring noises came from a water lily pond. They saw Hippo snoozing with only his head above the surface. He opened one eye. '*Um* – Rhino – come and – *er* – sit in here for a while. *Er* – it's very soothing for the bruises, it is.'

Rhino glared at him. And then the red faded from his eye. A rumble turned into a 'Good morning, how are you?' sort of noise.

Hippo blinked and a slow smile went all the way round his large mouth. '*Um* – a bad thing being tied up – *er* ...'

'Bad, very bad,' agreed Rhino. 'It took me a long time to see what Snake was up to.'

'*M-m-m-m*,' remarked Boohoo.

88

For a long time they lay in silence enjoying the cool softness of the mud. Boohoo moved his mouth close to Rhino's ear. 'Look over there – *um* ...'

Out of the bushes wriggled Snake. 'Good morning,' Snake spoke in his most soothing voice.

Rhino heaved himself out of the mud and Hippo followed more slowly.

'What a pity you didn't struggle a bit harder yesterday,' simpered Snake.

Rhino came a step closer. Thoughts were moving through his head faster than he ever remembered them moving before. He opened his mouth and said, loudly, 'No! You're wrong!'

Snake slid away into the shadows hissing to himself, 'I'll need to use a lot more cunning next time.'

Rhino started to think about Elephant. He shook his head to see if he was awake. The pain in his horn quickly told him that he was. He remembered the great rock, the anthill and the *buyu* tree.

Boohoo stood quietly on the edge of the mud. After a while he said, '*Um – er –* it's much better to listen to Elephant than to Snake, isn't it?'

Giraffe's head came down through the leaves, 'Snake still at it?' he asked.

Rhino nodded and Boohoo said slowly, '*Oh,* yes – *er –* he – *um ...*'

Twiga smiled. 'He spends his time whispering words that get others into trouble.'

'*Er –* yes,' said Boohoo. 'But – *um – er –* Elephant's different. He – *um –* spends his time getting others out of – *um –* trouble.'

'You're right,' grunted Rhino. 'Come and let's talk to him now.'

'Good,' said Antelope, prancing in front and talking over his shoulder. 'Do you remember the day when Elephant saved Jojo, the mongoose, from Hyena and his relations by tossing them out of the way with his tusks?'

Rhino stopped, 'Perhaps my horn could be useful.'

'It could, you know,' nodded Twiga, 'and your strength.'

Rhino walked on, his mind working busily. Before long they were all under the umbrella trees.

Rhino came close to Elephant and said, 'Thank you for what you did yesterday.' Then, in the quietest voice the jungle had ever heard him use, 'I've been thinking.' And he told Elephant about his horn and his strength and he finished up, 'perhaps these could be useful to you.' Again he felt the warm feeling as Elephant and he talked about what he could do and how Elephant wanted him to do it.

After a time Rhino and Hippo walked back to the water lily pond side-by-side. 'It's better to walk with Elephant and those that go his way,' said Rhino suddenly.

'Yes,' nodded Boohoo. 'Much better. Snake and – *er* – Hyena and –the others – very disagreeable.' Suddenly there was excitement in his voice. 'Did you hear Elephant say 'Resist Snake and he will go for his life?''

'I heard,' said Rhino. There was a movement in the grass. A glint came into his eye and he looked across and found to his surprise that both he and Hippo had the same idea.

'Good afternoon, Rhino,' hissed Snake softly. 'I was thinking that ...'

Rhino swung round, lifted both feet and came down – THUMP – where Snake had been a second before.

'Oh, good,' chuckled Boohoo. 'He understood that, *eh?*'

They watched the movements become less and less in the grass. Twiga stood beside them. 'That's wisdom. Not to listen to what Snake says is good, but not to give him the chance to say it is even better.'

Rhino nodded. He would remember. Deep inside him he knew that he had become a new rhinoceros.

'That doesn't often happen to rhinos,' said Kali.

'Truly,' agreed Daudi. 'But make no mistake; it often happens to men.'

'When they ask Jesus to forgive them and to take charge of their lives?' asked Tali.

'And the Bible says, "Therefore, if anyone is in Christ, he is a new creation," ' said Mgulu.

Elizabeti went on with the quotation, 'The old has gone, the new has come.' (2 Corinthians chapter 5 verse 17).

Lutu laughed. She slipped the bandage from her eyes. She walked round the wheelbarrow, avoided buyu roots and then stopped in front of Daudi.

'You can see!' shouted Kali and Tali.

'I can see,' nodded Lutu. 'First when I heard the story of blind monkey my inside eyes opened and now my ordinary ones see as well.'

Elizabeti whispered, 'The old has gone ...'

* * *

What's Inside the Fable?

Special message: If we ask Jesus to take charge of our lives, he makes us into a new creation.

Read *1 Peter 2:2*

Read *Acts 5:20*

Read *Romans 6:4*

GLOSSARY

JUNGLE DOCTOR'S WORDS AND NAMES
How to say them and what they mean

Animals	Pronunciation
Boohoo - hippo	Boohoo
Dic-Dic - antelope	Dickdick
Faru - rhino	Faroo
Goon - baboon	Goon
Jojo - mongoose	Joejoe
Koko - monkey	Cocoa
Lwalwa - tortoise	Lwalwa
Nzoka - snake	Nzoker
Stripey - zebra	Stripey
Tembo - elephant	Temboe
Toto - monkey	Toetoe
Twiga - giraffe	Twigger

Names	Pronunciation
Dan	Dan
Daudi	Dhawdee
Elizabeti	Elizabetee
Gulu	Gooloo
Kali	Karlee
Liso	Leesoo
Lutu	Lootoo
Mgulu	Mgooloo
Tali	Tarlee
Yuditi	Yooditee

Swahili	Pronunciation	English
Buyu	Booyoo	Baobab tree
Bwana	Bwarner	Sir, Mister, Lord
Kilele	Keylaylay	Noise

JUNGLE DOCTOR'S ANIMAL STORIES

Jungle Doctor's Fables
There was once a monkey who didn't believe in crocodiles.
ISBN: 978-1-84550-608-7

Jungle Doctor's Monkey Tales
Small monkeys never could remember not to get too near to the hind fee of zebra.
ISBN: 978-1-84550-609-4

Jungle Doctor's Tug-of-War
Even by monkey standards, Toto was pretty dim. The Jungle underworld think he will turn out to be easy meat.
ISBN: 978-1-84550-610-0

Jungle Doctor's Hippo Happenings
Boohoo the Unhappy Hippo had a great deal of empty space between his strangely-shaped ears.
ISBN: 978-1-84550-611-7

Jungle Doctor's Rhino Rumblings
Rhino has small eyes, a big body, a tiny brain, and a huge idea of his own importance.
ISBN: 978-1-84550-612-4

Jungle Doctor meets Mongoose
Again and again the snake struck, but the flying ball of fur with the fiery eyes always managed to jump backwards.
ISBN: 978-1-84550-613-1

CHRISTIAN FOCUS PUBLICATIONS

Christian Focus **Christian Heritage** **CF4K** **Mentor**

Christian Focus Publications publishes books for adults and children under its four main imprints: Christian Focus, CF4K, Mentor and Christian Heritage. Our books reflect that God's word is reliable and Jesus is the way to know him, and live for ever with him.

Our children's publication list includes a Sunday School curriculum that covers pre-school to early teens; puzzle and activity books. We also publish personal and family devotional titles, biographies and inspirational stories that children will love.

If you are looking for quality Bible teaching for children then we have an excellent range of Bible story and age specific theological books.

From pre-school to teenage fiction, we have it covered!

Find us at our web page:
www.christianfocus.com

CF4•K
*Because you're never
too young to know Jesus*